For Anna Barcock

A true friend

With love from Emma

ORCHARD BOOKS

338 Euston Road, London NW1 3BH

Orchard Books Australia

Level 17/207 Kent Street, Sydney, NSW 2000

First published in 2008 by Orchard Books

ISBN 978 1 84616 928 1

Text and illustrations © Emma Dodd 2008

A CIP catalogue record for this book
is available from the British Library.

1 3 5 7 9 10 8 6 4 2

Printed in Singapore

Orchard Books is a division of Hachette Children's Books,
an Hachette Livre UK Company.

I don't want a posh dog

Emma
Dodd

ORCHARD BOOKS

I don't want
a posh dog.

A blow-dry-when-washed dog.

I
don't
want a
patterned dog.
A jump-up-and-flatten

dog.

I don't **want** a handbag dog.

A tail-not-meant-to-wag dog.

I don't want
a snappy dog.

A growly,
never happy
dog.

I don't want
a gruff dog.

A grunty, wheezy,
puff dog.

I don't want a

speedy dog.

A greedy,

weedy,

needy dog.

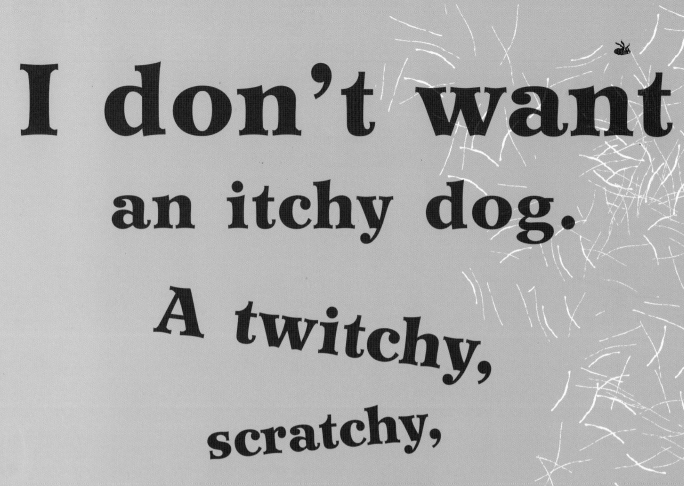

I don't want
an itchy dog.

A twitchy,

scratchy,

scritchy

dog.

I just want a silly dog.

A sweet, willy-nilly dog.

A not too proud or loud dog.

A know-me-in-the-crowd dog.

An
always keen
to try dog.

A dog I can call

My Dog.

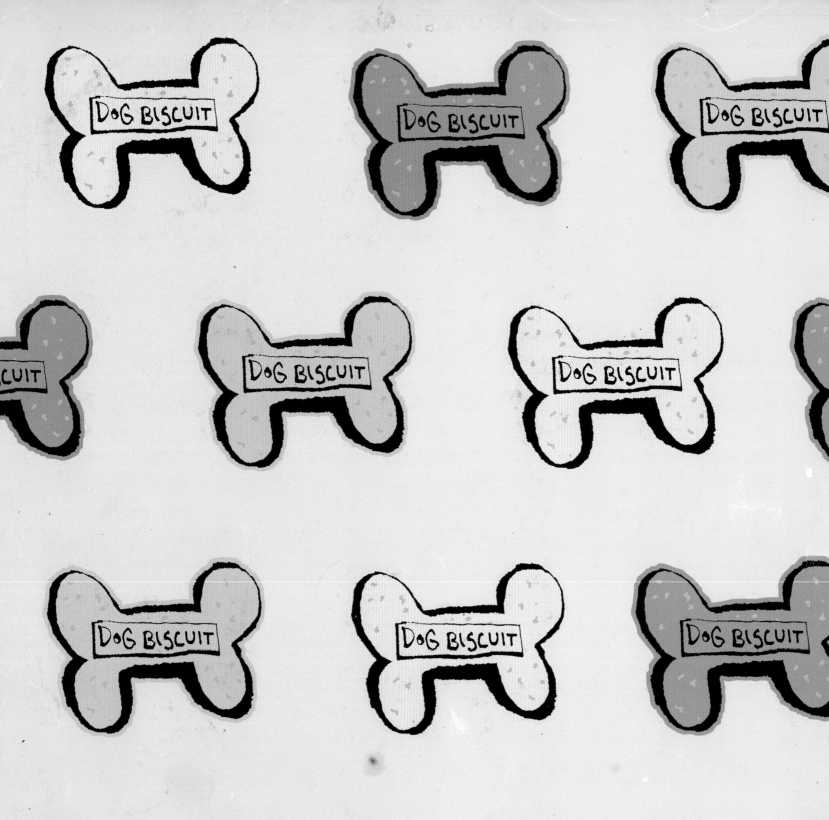